I0530973

Destiny's BIG CHANCE

Look for these and other books about Linelle Destiny in the Linelle Destiny Series:

Visit www.thesecretsistersclub.com

Linelle Destiny Series

Destiny's BIG CHANCE

Dr. Alicia Holland
Illustrations by Anoop PC

No parts of this book may be used or reproduced by any means, graphic, electronic, or mechanical, including photocopying, recording, taping or by any information storage retrieval system without the written permission of the author except in the case of brief quotations embodied in critical articles and reviews.

This book may be ordered through booksellers or by contacting:

iGlobal Educational Services, LLC
PO Box 94224
Phoenix, AZ 85070
www.iglobaleducation.com
512-761-5898

Because of the dynamic nature of the Internet, any web addresses or links contained in this book may have changed since publication and may no longer be valid. The views expressed in this work are solely those of the author and do not necessarily reflect the views of the publisher, and the publisher hereby disclaims any responsibility for them.

This is a work of fiction. Names, characters, businesses, places, events, and incidents are either the products of the author's imagination or used in a fictitious manner. Any resemblance to actual persons, living or dead, or actual events is purely coincidental.

Linelle Destiny Series: **Destiny's Big Chance**

Copyright © 2017 Alicia Holland, EdD. All Rights Reserved.

ISBN-13: 978-1-944346-17-1

Acknowledgements

I want to first honor God for placing in my heart to share my story with others. It was He whom brought Karen andI together to manifest this project.I am so grateful for Karen Hendry as she took my notes and helped write this fictitious book. There are truly no words to express my gratitude as you are truly a blessing.

I also want to thank Surendra Gupta for his creativity in formatting and Anoop PC for his creativity in bringing life to the designs and illustrations in this book series. Both of you are amazing!

Dedication

I dedicate this book series to my beautiful and talented daughters, Georgia and Amaiya Johnson. Remember, you are valued, loved, and competent. You are worthy!

Part 1:
Incredible Changes

Chapter 1
Job Offer

It's Monday morning. Destiny puts her back to the office door and pushes it open. *Two more weeks*, she thinks. Then she can have a break. It has been such a long year. After Wendy left the school last year, Destiny was given her workload as well. She has been dealing with both the Grade 5 Math and Science curriculum this whole school year, which is way more than one person should have to handle.

No one is in the office. Destiny reaches into her mailbox and finds a lone envelope. She looks at it and sees it's an envelope from the school board in Pflugerville.

Immediately, her heart starts beating a mile a minute. She is so tempted to open the envelope right then and there, but the school secretary, Patti, walks in at that moment.

"Good morning, Destiny," says Patti as she waters the plants on her desk. Patti is always so cheerful. Destiny doesn't think she has ever seen the woman frown, let alone seem upset or complain about anything. "Did you have a nice weekend?"

"Yes, well, busy," says Destiny as she tucks the envelope between the papers in her bag. "I don't get a lot of free time on the weekends."

"That tutoring center keeping you at it all through the weekend, is it?"

No, it's not the tutoring business, thinks Destiny. *It's the workload from this school that takes up all my time!* All she says is, "Yes,I guess so."

"Well, dear. You shouldn't work so hard.I hope you have some nice plans for summer. Take some time to get away?"

"Well, no plans, yet. But we'll see."

Destiny says goodbye and heads up to her classroom. She needs to get prepared for her day and with report cards due soon she doesn't have a lot of time to get anything else done. The envelope will have to wait.

The envelope did wait—until lunchtime. Destiny decides everything else can take a back seat and goes to the diner down the street to have lunch. When she gets there, she takes a nice sunny window seat.

Debbie, the regular lunchtime waitress comes over. "Howdy, Destiny. Nice to see you in today. The usual?"

"Hi, Debbie. Yes, please."

A couple of minutes later, a tall, cold glass of ice tea is placed on the table in front of her. Destiny takes a sip and then pulls the envelope out of her purse. Then she looks around to make sure no one from the school is there. The last thing she wants right now is for someone to see her and come over to chat.

With a deep breath, Destiny rips open the envelope and pulls out the letter inside. As she reads it, her heart starts beating again, as though it might burst out of her chest at any moment. She can barely sit still in her seat. In front of her is a job offer from the Pflugerville School Board!

Destiny was really hoping for a job offer. And it's a good one, too! She would be taking on a leadership role teaching math to middle school students at Diamond Back Middle School.

When her lunch arrives, she eats in a hurry.

"My Destiny," says Debbie. "You're quite a hurry today, aren't you."

"Yes, I am. I have an important phone call to make."

Debbie brings the bill and Destiny pays it. She leaves a good tip and goes outside. There is still 15 minutes left before she has to go back to the classroom and she is not going to miss the opportunity to get this job.

There is a park across the street. Destiny crosses and finds a bench to sit on. The bench has been painted by some neighborhood kids and it is full of colorful, cheerful flowers. The day is mostly sunny, with a few puffy clouds floating across the sky. They look like cotton balls way up there and Destiny feels she could float up there with them.

Once settled on the bench, Destiny pulls out the letter and her phone and calls the school number. On the fourth ring, someone answers.

"Hi, my name is Destiny Sycamores and I just received a job offer to teach at your school. I was wondering if I could speak with someone about it."

"Hello, Miss Sycamores. Yes, Principal Brandfather is in. Just one moment and I'll transfer you."

"Hello?" says a voice on the other end of the line, presumably Principal Brandfather.

"Hi, Principal Brandfather. This is Destiny Sycamores.I got a letter in the mail today offering me a teaching job at your school.I wanted to talk with you about it, if you have a moment."

"Yes, Destiny.I have your file right here in front of me, actually. Your resume is quite impressive. We would be pleased to have someone with your abilities and experience teaching at our school."

"That's great," replies Destiny. "I would absolutely love to come and teach there."

"That's wonderful. ThenI assume you are taking the position?"

"Oh, yes!"

"Wonderful!I will do up the paperwork and have it sent over. Consider it on its way."

"Thank you so much," says Destiny. "I look forward to meeting you soon."

"As do I, Destiny. Thanks for calling."

Destiny hangs up and does a little dance with her feet as she contains a whoop of joy and excitement. She can barely hold it in, but since she needs to get back to the school, she needs to calm herself.

She breathes deeply and starts to walk back to the school. By the time she gets there, she has composed herself and is ready for the afternoon.

Later that day, Destiny opens her apartment door and rushes inside. It's been all she can do to stay focused all afternoon. Of course, when she is with her students, Destiny is fully absorbed in teaching them, but when they aren't her focus, she can't keep her mind off her new job.

Despite her excitement, Destiny realizes there are things she needs to consider if she is going to be teaching in Pflugerville. It would be a too far a commute from Hutto, which is where she lives now. That means she is very likely going to have to move.

Moving means finding a new place to live, packing, and organizing everything, and on top of that, she will be preparing for her new job. Clearly, Destiny knows what she will be doing this summer, after all.

But Destiny doesn't mind, not one bit. The position at the Pflugerville School is a dream come true. It is exactly the type of teaching position she has wanted since she began teaching.

Destiny pulls out a pad of paper and a pen and begins to make a list. She needs to start getting organized. *Pflugerville, hereI come!*

Chapter 2
Saying Goodbye

Destiny peeks into Principal Limestone's office before heading up to her classroom. It's Wednesday morning on the last week of school. It took a whole week for the paperwork for Destiny's new job to arrive. She had actually started getting nervous when it wasn't in her mailbox by Friday.

But it finally came and she filled it out and sent it in. Now that she has signed on the dotted line and her new job is official, it is time to tell Principal Limestone she is leaving. She even has a letter of resignation ready. But she is terribly nervous.

Destiny has always been nervous when the time comes to tell her boss she is leaving a job. She thinks back to when she left the job she had at the jewelry store back home. She had been terrified, but it was completely unfounded. She just hopes this will be as smooth and easy.

Principal Limestone is at her desk. "Hi Daniella," says Destiny. "Do you have a moment?"

"Hi, yesI do," she says, looking up from her desk.

"Okay, well,I just wanted to let you know that I'll be leaving. The school that is."

"Leaving?"

"Yes," says Destiny, handing Principal Limestone the letter she is carrying. "I have been hired for a position teaching math to middle school students at Diamond Back Middle School in Pflugerville. It's a great leadership role and right up my alley."

"I daresay it is," says Principal Limestone. "Well,I won't lie. I'm mighty sorry to see you go."

Her brow is furrowed and Destiny knows why. With her leaving, Principal Limestone is going to have to fill both math and science positions and that won't be easy. Chances are she won't find one person willing to do both, so she'll have to hire two teachers to replace Destiny. *As it should be,* Destiny thinks.

"Thank you," says Destiny. "I'll be sorry to leave.I love the kids here."

"Well, thank you, Destiny.I am very happy for you andI wish you the best of luck in your new position."

"Thanks," says Destiny. She leaves and when she gets out into the hallway, she breathes a deep sigh of relief. She is glad that's over.

She turns to head to the stairs when a woman's voice comes from behind her. "Excuse me, Miss Sycamores?"

Destiny turns and there is a woman approaching her. "Yes?"

"Hi, Miss Sycamores. My name is Raquel. I'm Randi's mother."

"Yes, hi, Raquel. And please, call me Destiny. Is there somethingI can do for you?"

"I really just wanted to say thank you for all you've done for Randi this year. His marks have gone up so much, but more importantly, his confidence has grown by leaps and bounds. It's just been an amazing transformation."

"Thank you so much," says Destiny. "I am glad he is doing so much better. He has worked hard and it has paid off. I'll miss him next year."

"Miss him?"

"Yes, I am moving to a new school. In Pflugerville."

"Oh," says Raquel. "Randi didn't tell me."

"I only just found out, so it's a bit new even for me."

"Pflugerville," says Raquel. "That's quite a commute from here."

"Yes, it is. I'm planning to move."

"Buying?"

"Yes, I hope to."

"Well, let me know if you need any help," says Raquel. "I'm a real estate agent and I know that area well." She hands Destiny her card. "It's the least I can do after what you've done for Randi.

"Thank you. Maybe we can get together and talk about what's available?"

Raquel nods. "Let's do tea. Friday evening? I can show you some prospects."

"Sounds great," says Destiny.

They say their goodbyes and Destiny heads to class, excited by everything that is happening in her life.

Wednesday and Thursday pass quietly, but they crawl at a snail's pace. Destiny has her report cards done by Thursday at lunchtime and it seems Friday might never come. But it does, and with it the school assembly.

The assembly is coming to a close, the students getting antsy. Principal Limestone goes up to the front of the gym and speaks. "There is one final announcement to make today before everyone goes back to class. It is with great sadness thatI tell you all that Miss Sycamores will be leaving us. She has been hired on by the Pflugerville School Board."

The students erupt with a sound louder than any Destiny has ever heard in the gym. It's almost deafening. Destiny can hear boos and shouts telling her to stay. She is overwhelmed with emotion and so touched that the students think so highly of her.

Principal Limestone motions for Destiny to come up front. When she does, everyone quiets down. "Thank you, all of you," says Destiny. "I am going to miss you all so much, but I'll check back to see how you're all doing. AndI want you to remember, you are loved, valued, and competent."

At that, everyone cheers. Even the teachers are cheering for her. Destiny can feel tears come to her eyes. It's not the last time she cries that day.

It was tough to leave her students at the end of the day. Sitting in the tea shop, waiting for Raquel, Destiny thinks about it and smiles. She also feels the tears welling up again. Just then, Raquel walks in. *Just in time*, thinks Destiny.

They order their drinks and sit down. Destiny has a nice cup of tea. "You know," says Raquel, "Randi is so sad you are leaving.I just hope he'll be okay without you."

"Raquel, he'll be fine. He has everything within him to succeed in math. It was always there.I just pointed him in the right direction and I'm sure he can take it from here."

"Yes, I think you're right. And if you're not, I'll know where to find you," says Raquel with a wink.

She spreads out some options for Destiny to look at. Destiny browses through them, 12 in total.

"I wasn't sure exactly what you were looking for in a house, so I brought a wide selection."

"Well, I want a big yard for sure," says Destiny.

"That rules out these four," says Raquel, removing them from the pile.

"Hmmm," says Destiny. "I like the look of this one." It has a picture of a nice brick house.

"Okay. Well, if you like that one, you'll probably like this one." Raquel pulls a profile. "And this one." She pulls out another one.

Finally, Destiny has it narrowed down to four choices.

"These are great houses," says Raquel. "How about I arrange to see them this weekend? That way, you can get this part of your plans taken care of right away and can spend the rest of your summer getting ready for your move."

"That sounds great. Thank you so much!"

They finish their drinks and part ways. As she drives home, Destiny realizes she is about to go house hunting. She is amazed at how far she has come. Her own house! She can't wait to call and tell Momma!

Chapter 3

House Hunting

While most teachers are probably enjoying their first Saturday morning of summer vacation sleeping in, Destiny is up with the sun. How could she not be when she is destined to find her new home today?

Destiny makes a cup of tea and showers. Then she chooses a bright, sunny dress. It's yellow with blue flowers and it perfectly defines how she feels today.

Her stomach rumbles a little, but Destiny just wants to get on the road, so she decides she will get breakfast on the way out of town and eat it on the drive to Pflugerville. She has arranged to meet Raquel there at 9:00 AM and she doesn't want to be late.

The morning is clear and sunny, the air pleasantly warm. Destiny drives down the street and stops in at Round Rock Donuts. She gets another cup of tea and a cinnamon roll to eat during the drive.

The drive is wonderful. Destiny feels so free as she flies along the highway. It's like nothing can possibly hold her down. It's only 20 minutes to get to Pflugerville, and as she drives into town she can see a lot of new housing developments under construction. It is clear Pflugerville is expanding quickly, but these newer houses don't appeal to Destiny.

As she gets further into town, Destiny begins to see some of the older neighborhoods. The houses are lovely, well-landscaped, and well-kept. Many of them have covered porches on the front and beautiful flower gardens. It feels very homey and Destiny knows she will love living here.

When she finds the real estate office where she is meeting Raquel, Destiny finds she is a half an hour early. She parks on the street and finishes her cinnamon roll while she waits. Then, with a few minutes left to spare, Destiny decides to take a short walk down the street, just to see what downtown Pflugerville is like.

At nine o'clock, Destiny pushes the door to the real estate office open and steps inside. Raquel is sitting at a small table in the office and she looks up as Destiny enters.

"Good morning!" greets Raquel. "Are you ready to find your dream home today?"

"I sure am!" Destiny replies.

"Great. We can take my car. I'm parked just down the street a ways."

Raquel picks up a folder that is lying on the table in front of her, shoulders her purse, and the two women go outside and walk down the street to Raquel's car. It's a shiny new, Honda in a nice tone of blue.

As Raquel pulls out and starts to drive down the street, Destiny says, "This is such a nice town. I really feel at home here."

"It is lovely, isn't it?" says Raquel. "I've considered moving here myself, butI don't want to take Randi away from his school and his friends. He's happy there."

"I can understand that," says Destiny.

Five minutes later, they pull up in front of the first house on the list. Raquel gets the key out of the lock box and unlocks the door. They walk through and Destiny really likes the kitchen. The house is spacious, with three bedrooms, but only one bathroom. The backyard is a decent size, but not what she had imagined.

The next two houses are also very nice, but neither of them really feels right to Destiny. They have some nice features, an en suite bathroom in one, a bigger back yard in the other. But Destiny knows they have saved the best for last. The final house is the one that looked the best on paper and Destiny just hopes it lives up to her expectations.

When they arrive, she knows the house is the right one before she sets foot inside the door. Inside, the house is a dream. With an open-concept layout, five bedrooms, three bathrooms, and a huge backyard, it is everything Destiny wants in a house.

"Oh, Raquel," says Destiny. Then she doesn't know what else to say. She is speechless.

"I figured you would like this one the best," says Raquel.

"Oh,I do. This is the oneI want. There's no question."

"Okay," says Raquel. "Let's head back to the office. There is paperwork to take care of."

Ten minutes later, the two women arrive back at the real estate office. They stand outside the office and Raquel says, "Destiny,I will draw up the paperwork and drop by your apartment this evening so you can sign everything."

"That sounds great," says Destiny.

They say goodbye and part ways. The drive home feels so surreal to Destiny. She is excited and nervous. Nervous about the commitment she is about to make and nervous that her offer won't be accepted. Only time will tell, though. But to keep her mind off things, Destiny decides to go to the mall and get some lunch and do some shopping.

Destiny watches Raquel as she lays out the paperwork in front of her. They are sitting at Destiny's kitchen table. Raquel has printed out the offer on the house and there are pages and pages in front of her.

"I didn't realize how much paper was involved when you buy a house," says Destiny.

"Oh, there is plenty of paperwork. And this is just the offer. Wait until you get to the purchasing paperwork."

"Oh, wow," says Destiny.

After a couple of minutes, Raquel says, "Okay, now you need to initial here, here, and here. Oh and here." She points at places where there is a small X marked on the pages. "And you need to sign and date here and here."

Destiny reads through the offer, which takes a few minutes, and initials and signs where she needs to. When she is finished, she sets the pen down on the table and takes a deep breath. "Now what?"

"Now, I send this through to the seller's agent and they decide whether to accept your offer or give you a counter offer. You have only asked for a price slightly under their listing price and you have asked for the appliances and window coverings. That is fairly standard soI don't see any real issues there. You do want a relatively quick closing, so hopefully they are okay with that."

"When will we know their answer?" asks Destiny.

"Well, it is the weekend, so it could be as late as Monday, but if they are keen to sell,I suspect we will hear back sooner than that."

"I hope so," says Destiny. "I don't thinkI can stand waiting very long. It's pure torture!"

"Well,I will send this to the agent as soon asI leave here andI promiseI will call you as soon asI hear anything at all."

"Thank you so much, Raquel."

"Now try to get some sleep," says Raquel.

"Not sure that will happen, but I'll try."

When Raquel is gone, Destiny turns on the TV and finds a movie to watch. It's something to take her mind off the waiting. She feels wide awake and is up until 1:00 AM watching television. When she goes to bed, it's hard to fall asleep, but she eventually drifts off.

At eight o'clock the next morning, Destiny wakes to the sound of her phone ringing. At first she considers ignoring it and going back to sleep, then she realizes who it is calling her so early on a Sunday morning.

Destiny jumps out of bed and races to the phone. "Hello," she says, a little out of breath.

"Destiny?" says Raquel on the other end of the line. "I have good news for you. Your offer has been accepted!"

"Really?" says Destiny. "That's wonderful! Oh my! What do we do now?"

"I'll drop by later today with all the paperwork for the sale. You'll need to settle things at the bank tomorrow. And then, well, you had better start packing."

"Oh, definitely! Thanks again and I'll see you later."

When she hangs up, Destiny stands there for a moment, processing everything that has happened. She is stunned. She will be moving once again, but this time into the house of her dreams!

Destiny heads to her bedroom to get dressed. No going back to sleep now. It's time to get moving. She needs to get some boxes so she can start packing and there's no time like the present.

Part 2:
Summer Excitement

Chapter 4

Doctor Destiny!

✧ ✧ ✧

Destiny is on her lunch break. Principal Brandfather asked her to help run the summer program and she couldn't refuse her new boss, so here she is working away. Since she hasn't moved yet, Destiny has been commuting every day. This has left her very little time to pack and prepare for her move.

However, she is enjoying the kids immensely and she knows it will all work out fine in the end. At least she will be moved and settled by the time the school year begins.

During her lunch break, Destiny decides to browse the Internet, just for something to do. She is poking around the various local universities, just to see what they have to offer. Destiny is more curious than anything, with no real goal in mind, but she comes across a school called Nova Southeastern University. It stands out to her because it has the same acronym—NSU—as the school at which she got her first degree.

Huh, thinks Destiny. She becomes more curious and starts looking through their doctoral programs. There is one in education that looks really good so she looks at the requirements. She is surprised to find that she qualifies for the program.

Destiny is very tempted to apply, but does she really have time to work on another degree? Especially one that is so demanding? She is about to move into a new home and start a new school year at a new school. Plus, her tutoring business is growing like crazy. Every month, Destiny has more students signing up for her services.

Destiny stares at the screen. She stares at the button that says Registration. She hovers the mouse over the button and a little voice inside her head says to go for it. So, she clicks on the Registration button and finds the application for the program. She prints it out. She might be crazy, but she feels this is the right decision.

It isn't until Destiny gets home that evening that she is able to look over the application. It is quite intensive and she knows it will take her a while to fill out. At least it's Friday, so she doesn't have to get up as early as usual tomorrow morning. The tutoring center doesn't open until 1:00 PM and she has someone to cover for her if she can't make it in.

After a quick dinner of leftover soup from the day before, Destiny sits at her desk and begins to look over what she needs for the application. She needs a copy of her previous degree, the application form, details of her work experience, and two professional references.

Destiny thinks for a moment. Obviously, the best references would be her two former supervisors, Principal Easton and

Principal Limestone. She just hopes they will say good things about her and that they will reply quickly.

Destiny gets online and sends an email to each of them. With that done, she begins to fill out the application. It is very detailed and it takes her a couple of hours to get it all filled out and all the relevant material gathered.

Destiny has some copies of her degree and transcript. She always keeps them on hand in case she needs them for anything and she is immensely grateful that she plans ahead. As long as her references come through quickly, she should be able to get her application in by early next week.

Once finished, Destiny stands up, stretches, and looks at the boxes scattered around her home. Some are empty, some partially full. She is running out of time and she needs to get packing. She spends the next two hours packing and gets a lot accomplished.

Exhausted, she practically falls onto her couch, thinking it must be about time to go to bed. Then she remembers the references she is waiting for. It wouldn't hurt to check and see if either of the principals has gotten back to her so Destiny logs into her email.

Sure enough, there are two new emails, one from Principal Easton and one from Principal Limestone. Destiny looks at each of the reference letters. Everything they have written is nothing but positive, glowing reports of Destiny's ability to work with students, remain professional, and go above and beyond.

Destiny prints out the two reference letters, gathers the application and everything she needs to include with it, and puts it all into a large envelope. She is done! She stamps and addresses the envelope, puts on her shoes, and steps outside. If she puts it in the mailbox tonight, it will be picked up tomorrow.

The sun is setting and it is a beautiful summer evening. Destiny hurries to the mailbox on the corner down from her place. She opens the little door, which squeaks slightly in protest, and slips the envelope in. She can hear it slide down the chute and hit the bottom with a small, but satisfying thud.

With a smile on her face, Destiny enjoys a slow walk back home. So many exciting developments in her life. It can't possibly get any better.

Destiny is bleary eyed when she wakes up the next morning. She had a hard time getting to sleep the night before because her mind was racing about her possible new degree and her new home and everything else going on in her life. In fact, all that thinking led her to consider her tutoring center.

She has been leasing space from Nichole for a while now, but Nichole recently raised her rent. It was clear Destiny's business was doing well and it is also clear that Nichole thought she should benefit from that success. Nichole has been great, but between the higher rent and the need for a larger space, it is time for Destiny to start looking for a different location for her tutoring center.

Destiny goes to the kitchen and makes a cup of tea. Then, still cozy in her pajamas, she logs onto her computer and starts looking at the options for new office space. She wants to find something for a comparable price to what she is paying Nichole, but she needs the space to be a good size and in a central location.

As she is poking around, Destiny runs across some information on an available government contract that will see tutoring services go into area schools. Destiny takes a look at the requirements for the contract. It is immediately clear to Destiny that Get Your Mind Right Tutoring is just what the government needs.

Destiny doesn't hesitate. If she can get this contract, it would mean big and wonderful things for her business. Just like with her doctoral application, this one is quite lengthy. It takes Destiny close to two hours to fill it out and gather all the supporting documentation, but she gets it done. Then she throws on some clothes and goes down to the mailbox she visited only the evening before and sends it off.

Once she is back from the mailbox, she looks at the clock. It's 11:30. She calls into the center to let them know she won't be in today, but to call her if they need anything.

Destiny really needs to get packing. Her move date is coming up fast and she is nowhere near ready. As she starts packing some of her extra dishes, Destiny thinks about her life. Things seem to be falling into place so easily, the timing so perfect. If everything comes through, she is going to be busy, but Destiny thrives on being busy. That's when she does her best work. *Bring it on,* she thinks. *I can handle it!*

Chapter 5
The Move

The big day has arrived. Destiny has been working like crazy to get ready. It is now moving day and her stress is at peak levels. She is ready, but just barely, having gotten up and packed the last few boxes early this morning. And on top of getting ready to move, she had to go out and find a new space for her tutoring center last week. She has to go check it out today.

When the movers arrive, Destiny is standing on her doorstep ready and waiting. The driver of the truck gets out and walks up to her, while the other two movers go into the house.

"Howdy, Ma'am. You Miss Sycamores?"

Destiny nods.

"My name's Jeb," says the driver, extending his hand. "You all set for us?"

Destiny shakes Jeb's hand. "Hi, Jeb. Yes, everything is ready."

"That's fine," says Jeb. "Now, it'll take us a couple of hours at least to load everything up, depending on how much you have."

"Okay. I am hoping you'll be done by 11:00 at the latest. I have tenants coming to move in and I expect them late this morning. Is that going to be possible?"

"We'll do our best, Ma'am." Just then one of the other movers comes out of the house and says, "It looks good. Maybe two and a half to three hours."

Jeb nods. "We are gonna try to get it wrapped up in two and a half for the lady here. Think we can make that happen?"

"We'll sure try," says the other mover and he nods to Destiny and walks back into the house.

"That there's Danny. He's a good guy. The other's Mike. I can't make any promises, but we'll work hard to get it done in time for ya."

"Thank you, Jeb," says Destiny. "I really appreciate it."

Jeb nods his head and gets to work. Destiny watches as they slowly pack her entire life into the moving truck, offering them some cola she is keeping in a cooler when it is clear they are getting hot.

When the movers have everything loaded in, it is 10:55. Destiny's new tenants haven't arrived yet and she breathes a sigh of relief.

Jeb comes over to Destiny and says, "We are all ready to go, Ma'am. Got it done in the nick of time, I'd say."

"You did just fine," says Destiny.

"Now, are you planning on following us there?"

"Not right away, no," says Destiny. "I have to wait for my new tenants and then I have a stop to make on my way there. But here are the keys and you have the address, right?"

Jeb nods, taking the keys. "Yup, we know where we're heading. Now, it won't take as long to unload as it did to load. Maybe about half the time."

"I'll be there in time," says Destiny, hoping she didn't just tell the biggest fib of her life.

"Sounds good, Ma'am. See you soon."

As the moving truck pulls out, Destiny prays silently that her tenants show up soon. As though her prayers were heard, it is less than five minutes later that another moving truck pulls in, followed by a small blue Ford.

Destiny greets the tenants, Amanda and Greg, and they thank her for the keys. "We are so happy to have this house," says Amanda. "This is going to make a great home, at least until we can afford to buy our own."

"I'm very glad," says Destiny. Then she wishes them luck settling in and gets into her car. She needs to make a stop in Round Rock before she heads to her new house.

About 20 minutes later, Destiny is unlocking the door to her new office space. She had seen it briefly the week before and signed the lease agreement on the spot, and now that she is walking in, she hopes she didn't make a mistake.

But when she gets inside, she is very pleased with the space. It is so big. There is plenty of room for all of her students and then some. She can spread them out, have different sections and groups. And there is plenty of room for tables, shelves, and desks. Plus, she has a separate office in the back and there is a reception area at the front. The space couldn't be more perfect.

Destiny looks at her watch. She has an hour tops before the movers are finished. Just then, a knock comes at the door of the office. A young woman is standing outside. Destiny opens the door and welcomes her. "Hi there. I'm Destiny Sycamores. And you are?"

"Shelly. Shelly Franklin."

"Pleased to meet you, Shelly. Sorry, butI am expecting another applicant andI didn't know which one you were."

"That's just fine," says Shelly.

"Unfortunately,I have nowhere for us to sit, yet," says Destiny, "but let's get started while we wait for Annalise.I could see by your resume that you have a lot of experience working with learners with special needs."

"Yes,I have been working with special needs learners in a couple of our local schools for the past four years now. Working with these kids has been the highlight of my career."

"And you have had a lot of success?"

"Oh, yes. Every one of my students has improved in their reading by at least two grade levels andI have helped 50% of them to reach grade level within two years."

"That's very impressive," says Destiny as she notices another young woman walking up to the door. Destiny motions for her to come on in.

"You must be Annalise," says Destiny, extending her hand.

"Yes, Ma'am," says Annalise. "Annalise McGrary, at your service." She shakes Destiny's hand and Destiny feels that she might shake it right off.

"Shelly, Annalise andI have already spoken quite a lot over the phone, butI wanted the two of you to meet, since you will be working together. Annalise is a writing coach who also works with special needs students in high school and college, whichI think will pair very nicely with a reading specialist."

"Does that meanI have the job?" asks Shelly.

"It sure does," says Destiny with a smile.

"I know we'll get along so well," says Annalise, giving Shelly a hug.

"Wow. Uh yeah," says Shelly, hugging her back. "I'm sure we will."

"Well, ladies," says Destiny. "I am afraidI don't have more time to talk with you. Today is moving day for me andI need to get there before the movers are done. But if you have time, you can maybe get tea or tea somewhere and chat."

"I can do that," says Annalise, nodding her head and smiling.

"I have some time, too," says Shelly.

"Great," says Destiny.

The three of them walk outside and Destiny locks the door behind them. As she bids them goodbye and they walk away down the sidewalk, Destiny can hear Annalise going on about the work they can do with the kids at the center. Destiny smiles as she walks to her truck.

Destiny pulls up in front of her new house. It's as beautiful and amazing as she remembers. She can see them carrying her sofa into the house, which means they are almost finished because they are unloading the large furniture. She breathes a sigh of relief at making it on time. It seems today is a day of cutting it close.

As she stands on her front lawn, a voice speaks from behind her. "You must be the new neighbor."

Destiny turns around to see a man crossing the street to greet her.

"Yes, I'm Destiny Sycamores."

"Pleased to meet ya, Destiny. I'm Darryl Wintersby, your neighbor across the way. Good to have you, good to have you."

"Thank you, Darryl."

"And what is it you do for a living?"

"I'm a teacher."

"What a noble profession, guiding our young minds and making good citizens out of them. Much better than the last people who lived in this house. He managed a grocery store, but they closed down his location. And she was a clerk at a law firm. They didn't socialize much. Never understood why. Everyone knows everyone in this neighborhood."

"Oh, yes, well, I'm happy to get to know everyone," says Destiny.

"Well, that's good. We don't need snobby neighbors around here. The only one we have is Mable, who has lived here longer than anyone else on this block. She is a right bit cranky, so watch out for her."

"Thanks for the heads up," says Destiny, but red flags are going up. Darryl seems to know everyone's business and he is clearly very judgemental. Not at all the type of person Destiny likes to associate with. But he is her neighbor so she should make an effort. "And what do you do?"

"Me, oh, I'm home most of the time. Injured my back at work and can't do the manual labor I used to do. Was in construction. Just drive on over to the next subdivision. I built those houses, before my injury. The wife, she works though. A real estate agent. She sold this house for the previous couple."

"That's wonderful. I look forward to meeting her." just then, Jeb comes out of the house and starts walking toward her. "I think I'm needed with the movers so if you'll excuse me."

"Oh, sure," says Darryl. "Now don't be a stranger." And then he is gone, back across the street.

Destiny speaks with Jeb, signs some papers, and hands him a check. She is sure she can see Darryl peeking out from behind his living room curtains, watching everything.

Once the movers have gone, Destiny goes inside her new home. All around her are boxes. It feels like there are more than there were this morning, like they multiplied in the moving truck on the way over.

Well, the first order of business is to get something to eat. Destiny realizes it is past lunchtime and she really didn't eat breakfast because she was scrambling to be ready for the movers.

Destiny searches through three boxes before finding her phone. She plugs it into the wall, hoping her service has been hooked up, and as soon as she does the phone rings. "Hello?"

"Destiny, girl," says Momma. "It's about time you answered."

"Momma, the movers just left."

"You all moved in then?"

"Yes, Momma, but I'm facing a pile of boxes."

"Well now, you'll get through that, honey. But don't forget to eat something. You need your strength."

"I know, Momma. I was just about to order pizza."

"Pizza?" shouts Momma, and Destiny is sure she could probably hear Momma without the phone. "That ain't healthy enough. You need some real food."

"Well, all my dishes are packed and I need to go shopping. I just moved, Momma." Momma has been in the same house for nearly 40 years. She doesn't remember what it's like to move.

"Alright, alright," says Momma. "Go order your pizza. But call me tomorrow and let me know how you makin' out."

"I will, Momma."

Destiny says goodbye and hangs up. Then she dials for pizza. Once she has ordered it, she stands and looks at the boxes. At least she labeled them all so they were put in the right rooms. She should start with the kitchen and get the refrigerator stuff put away. Then she can make up her bed. Destiny has a couple of days to unpack so she will set things to rights before she has to go to work.

Chapter 6

Acceptance

The Monday after the move, Destiny is working on unpacking when she sees the mail carrier walking down her front walkway toward the sidewalk. Destiny goes out to get the mail. She is hoping for something exciting, but not really expecting it. She still hasn't heard back about the doctoral program or the government contract.

She pulls the mail out of the box and starts to sift through it as she stands on her front step. Junk, junk, junk. She is about to give up on the mail that day when at the bottom of the pile is a letter, and it's from the university.

Destiny rushes into the house and drops the rest of the mail on the table next to the door. Then she starts dancing around the house, through the living room, into the kitchen, and back into the front hallway. She is so happy! She rips open the envelope and starts reading.

"Dear, Ms. Sycamores. We are delighted to inform you that you have been accepted into the education doctoral program at Nova Southeastern University."

Destiny starts dancing around the house again. How exciting! She is going to be Dr. Destiny! She keeps reading.

"Please fill out the enclosed paperwork and send in your registration for the Orientation session. We look forward to seeing you next week."

"Next week?" Destiny shouts out loud. She has to go to the school next week? "But that's in Florida," Destiny says to the empty house around her. She has to go to Fort Lauderdale, Florida next week! She had better call Calix and let him know. He will have to book time off work if he is going with her.

She picks up the phone and dials Calix's work number. When he answers, she just jumps right in. "Oh, Calix! I got accepted! I did it!"

"Slow down! Got accepted for what?"

"The doctoral program."

"That's great news!" says Calix. "We will celebrate when I get home."

"Okay, but there's something else. They expect me to attend the orientation session, which is next week."

"You have to be in Florida next week?"

"Yes. I know it's short notice, but I was hoping you could get the time off and come with me. It would be a nice trip before the school years starts and I get super busy."

"I would love to go with you. Let me talk to Dave and see what I can do. Maybe he can swing letting me go for a few days since things are starting to slow down now."

"Thanks!" says Destiny. They say their goodbyes and hang up. Destiny gets some paper and a pen. Time to make some travel plans.

✧ ✧ ✧

The following Saturday, Destiny and Calix pack up the truck and hit the road. It's raining, but that doesn't dampen Destiny's spirits. And by mid-day, the rain is gone, the roads dry up, and the sun comes out.

It's close to 1:00 pm when they get off the highway. Destiny sighs as Calix pulls into a parking space. They are stopping for lunch in a small town outside of Lafayette, Louisiana.

"What's the matter?" asks Calix.

"I just feel bad that we're passing so close to home and can't stop in for a visit."

"I know," he says. "It would be nice to see the family. Let's go get some lunch."

"Okay."

They go inside and a waitress named Doris shows them to a table. Destiny orders ice tea and Calix orders a Coke. They look through the menu in silence and when Doris brings their drinks, they each order a sandwich. Destiny's is a fried crab sandwich and Calix orders a roast beef sandwich.

After they order, Calix asks, "Are you excited?"

"Absolutely!I can't wait to get into it. There is so much to explore in a doctoral program. Choosing a topic will be hard, butI have a few ideasI want to run by my advisor."

"That's great. But you'll be so busy. Make sure you have time for me once in a while."

"Of course," says Destiny, reaching out and touching Calix's hand. "I always have time for you. We should make a date night. One day a week when I'm not allowed to work on anything and we do something special together."

"That sounds like a good idea," says Calix. "We can take turns choosing what we do and I'll go first."

"Deal," says Destiny.

They chat about some date night ideas and what they want to do while they are in Florida. Soon they are back on the road. After an overnight stay in Pensacola, Florida, they drive on through and reach Fort Lauderdale at dinner time on Sunday.

Destiny checks them into their hotel room and they take their luggage up. Then they order room service and watch television. They are just too tired from the drive to do anything else and Destiny has to be well-rested tomorrow for orientation.

Orientation runs over two days and Destiny enjoys meeting the faculty and some of the other students enrolling in the PhD program. Two of the students she meets are also doing PhDs in education. One is Sarah, who lives in Fort Lauderdale, and the other is Oliver, who is from Louisville, Kentucky.

After being greeted on the first day, Destiny attends a few general information sessions about the program and expectations. During one of the afternoon sessions, Destiny learns that she will be expected to spend her summers on campus in order to meet the residency requirements.

That evening, Destiny tells Calix this news over dinner. "Will we be able to manage that? I have to do it for three summers," she says.

"We'll figure it out," says Calix. "I have the summers off anyway, so I can come with you. Actually, it would make a nice getaway for a few weeks each year."

"Thank you," says Destiny. Calix is being so supportive and Destiny really appreciates it.

Tuesday morning, Destiny shows up at 9:00 and is greeted by a very tall, thin man, with hair nearly as thin as he is. "Hello, Destiny. I'm Dr. Larry Dewayne Carter andI am your doctoral supervisor."

"It's nice to meet you Dr. Carter.I am so excited about this program."

"I'm glad to hear it. AndI see you have a lot of experience already. You teach *and* run a tutoring center?"

"Yes."

"Your husband must be very supportive."

When Destiny looks confused, he nods at the ring on her finger. "Oh, yes. He is. Very."

"Children?"

"No, not yet. We just got married four months ago and it's too early for that."

"Well, children are a handful. ThatI can attest to," says Dr. Carter. "So what is it you were thinking of as your PhD focus?"

"I really want to focus on leadership. ButI am also very interested in curriculum development. Is there a wayI can combine the two of those?"

"You can do a major and a minor. That way you can work both aspects into your PhD."

"That would work.I was thinking about Organizational Leadership as the primary focus. So Curriculum Development would be the minor."

"I think we can accommodate that," says Dr. Carter. "Why don't you come to my office and we will look at some additional paperwork for you and start digging up some resources."

"Lead the way," says Destiny.

Later that day, Calix meets Destiny on campus. "How did it go?" he asks.

"It was wonderful! Just perfect.I am going to be able to research exactly whatI want. Dr. Carter, that's my supervisor, has set me up with a bunch of resources to get started.I have to draw up a work schedule and submit it to him by the end of next week, then we can get to it."

"Does that mean you're all mine this evening?" says Calix with a devilish grin on his face.

"It most certainly does," answers Destiny. "What did you have in mind?"

"I was thinking dinner and a stroll along the beach."

"You read my mind."

They have dinner at a lovely beachside restaurant set on the beach where they enjoy the catch of the day and a beautiful view of the ocean.

The next day, they drive down to Miami and spend two days soaking up the sun. Destiny knows it is a good idea to take some time with Calix and to just relax. Soon enough, she will be swimming in work and school.

But then she will become Dr. Destiny and the thought of that sends shivers up her spine. Destiny is very content on the drive back to Texas. She spent a wonderful week with her husband and is beginning a new journey in life. What could be better?

Part 3:
School Begins

Chapter 7
Jumbled Job

Destiny balances a box loaded with things for her classroom on her left hip while she opens the door to the school office. She is still exhilarated from her trip to Florida and she still feels relaxed. There is an entire week until school begins, but her summer has been so busy with the move, moving the tutoring office, and the trip to Florida that Destiny has not had time to create her lesson plans or prepare for her new leadership position.

The office is empty. Destiny looks in her mailbox, but it's just as empty as the office. Just then, a voice comes from behind her, "Ah, Destiny. I'm glad you're here," says Principal Brandfather. "CanI have a word?"

"Sure," says Destiny, wondering how Principal Brandfather snuck up on her like that. She puts her box on the counter in the school office and follows Principal Brandfather into her office.

Principal Brandfather gestures to a table in the corner of her office and she and Destiny take a seat.

Principal Brandfather shifts uncomfortably before she begins talking. "I wanted to let you know we have had to make some changes to your position here."

Oh no, thinks Destiny. *Not again.*

"Now, you will still be in a leadership position and helping to develop curriculum," Principal Brandfather rushes on in the wake of Destiny's silence. "And you will still be teaching math, but we need to shift you to a different focus—our special education and ESL students."

"I see," says Destiny, as she sighs a little too loudly.

"I can see you're disappointed," says Principal Brandfather. "I understand that, but we really need you in this position. You are the best suited for the task at hand."

"No,I understand andI love working with special needs and ESL students.I was just really looking forward to the opportunity to work with campus leadership. WillI still be able to?"

"I'm afraid not, at least not right now. Your focus is completely different. But you will still be teaching one higher level class."

"That's good," says Destiny.

Principal Brandfather smiles. "I'm glad you can see the benefits of working with our more needy students. We really are so happy to have you aboard."

"AmI in the same classroom?" asks Destiny.

"No, you have been assigned room 201," says Principal Brandfather, handing Destiny a key. "It's all cleared out and ready for you to make it your own."

"Thank you," says Destiny as she stands up. "I'd better get going.I have a lot of work to do to prepare for next week."

"I'm sure you will be well prepared when the students arrive. And thanks again for your understanding."

Destiny picks up her box on the way out of the office and makes her way upstairs. She finds her room and unlocks the door. It's a nice big room with a desk near the window. At least something has gone right today.

Destiny is unpacking the box she brought in when a knock comes at her classroom door. She looks up and there is a short, plump woman standing in the doorway. She looks to be in her mid- to late-40s, her black hair a little wild.

"Hello," says Destiny.

"Oh, hi. You must be our new team member." The woman walks across the room and holds out her hand. "My name is Ethel andI am one of the math teachers here."

Destiny shakes Ethel's hand. "Nice to meet you, Ethel. I'm Destiny."

"Oh,I know who you are. You're reputation precedes you, my dear. AndI am very much looking forward to working with you."

"Well, thank you, Ethel," says Destiny, wondering how her reputation is such common knowledge. She didn't even know she had a reputation. "What grade do you teach?"

"I teach sixth grade math. The other grade six math teachers are Richard, MiYaghi, and Rashema. ButI suspect you'll be working with more than just us, with curriculum development being a part of your new job here."

"Yes,I supposeI will," says Destiny. "I do look forward to that.I love developing curriculum. One of my favorite things."

"Well, honey,I won't keep you.I know you need to settle in and have a lot to do, but if you need anything, you just let me know, you hear? I'm just down the hall in 210."

"Thank you very much," says Destiny.

What a nice lady, thinks Destiny as she watches Ethel leave. Destiny feels a little better knowing she has some great teachers to work with. Maybe this won't be so bad after all.

About 20 minutes after Destiny gets home that day, her doorbell rings. Destiny answers the door to find Katie standing outside with a small gift bag in her hand.

"Katie! It's so good to see you." Destiny gives her friend a big hug. "Come on in."

Katie comes in and takes off her shoes. "Oh, Destiny, this house is amazing!" This is the first time Katie has been able to come out and see the house. She is staring around, wide-eyed. "There is so much space!I love how open it is and how much light you get."

"Thanks.I love it here."

"Oh, this is for you and Calix," says Katie, handing the gift bag to Destiny. "Just a little housewarming gift."

"You shouldn't have," says Destiny reaching inside the bag. She pulls out a beautiful candle holder. "Oh, it's lovely! AndI know just where to put it."

Katie follows Destiny as she walks over to a small table by the living room window. She places the candle holder on the table.

"Perfect," says Katie.

"Tea?" asks Destiny.

"Please."

They go into the kitchen and Katie sits at the table while Destiny fills the kettle. "Sorry about all the boxes," says Destiny.

"Calix has been working crazy hours and I've been so busy with everything that it is taking way longer thanI thought to unpack."

"Don't worry about it," says Katie. "It's not like this stuff is going anywhere. You have a lot on your plate right now."

"I know, butI don't like living out of boxes."

"You'll get it sorted. Now tell me about your PhD."

Destiny sets the tea on the table. "Well, there isn't much to tell at this point.I am in the initial stages, doing a literature review, so a lot of reading."

"Sounds thrilling," says Katie, a bit sarcastically.

Destiny smiles. "It *is* exciting. There have been a lot of cool improvements in curriculum development over the past 10 years."

"Yeah,I know. Just teasing."

"Do you want to stay and have dinner," asks Destiny. "Calix is working late so it would just be us."

"Sure, that would be nice."

"Great. I'll put on some water for pasta."

A half an hour later, after Destiny cooks shrimp Alfredo and Katie sets the table, the two friends are seated at the table once again. They have been having idle chit chat about how the start of their school year is going. Then Destiny says, "So what about outside of school? Seeing anyone?"

"Yes,I am!"

"Really? Who?"

"His name is Frank."

"How did you meet him?" Destiny is happy to hear her friend has found someone special.

"His wife works for me," says Katie.

"I don't understand. He's married?"

"Well, yes, right now he is. But he is going to divorce his wife and be with me. And I am going to adopt a child. He and I can be parents together."

Destiny is silent, her mind churning. Then she says, "Katie, taking someone's husband, well, it isn't very Christian."

"Well, I don't believe in God so I guess that isn't a problem."

"Oh," says Destiny, stunned. She doesn't know what else to say. God is such an important part of her life. She and Katie eat their last few bites in silence. Then Katie offers to help clean up.

"Oh, no. That's okay," says Destiny. "I can take care of it. Thank you, though."

"You sure?" asks Katie.

"Yeah, I am. I have to do some work unpacking and sorting things out in the kitchen anyway. Besides, you have a long drive home so you had better get going."

"Well, thanks for dinner," says Katie as Destiny walks her to the door.

"And thank *you* for the gift and the company," says Destiny. "Safe drive home."

They hug and Katie leaves. Destiny closes the door and then leans against it, her mind reeling. Has Katie really stolen someone's husband? What is she thinking? And she doesn't believe in God?

Destiny feels like Katie isn't the same person anymore, that she has changed. Or maybe this was always who she was and Destiny just didn't see it.

One thing is for sure, Destiny just cannot have people like that in her life, people who make bad decisions. These decisions end up going terribly wrong and a lot of drama results. Destiny has no time for Katie's drama. And she certainly doesn't want to be a party to this new relationship.

Destiny pushes herself away from the door. As she walks back to the kitchen to clean up, she knows she has to distance herself from Katie. She feels sad because she has been friends with Katie for such a long time, but she knows it is the best thing for her and her family.

Chapter 8
Acceptance

The school year has been moving along and it's late November now. Destiny arrives at school, and once in her classroom, pulls yesterday's mail from her bag. She was so busy yesterday and got home so late from the tutoring center that she didn't bother checking the mail. When she left this morning, she just pulled it out of the box and plopped it into her bag.

She begins sifting through the mail and one envelope catches her eye. It is from the government. She opens it up and finds a letter confirming that Get Your Mind Right Tutoring has won the government contract for tutoring in the schools.

Destiny jumps up from her desk with a whoop. It had been so long since she applied that she had long since given up on getting the contract. She had no idea it took them so long to go through the process of selecting an applicant.

Ethel pops her head into the classroom. "DidI hear some shouting in here?"

"Oh, yes, sorry ifI was too loud," says Destiny. "I just got some good news."

"Oooh! What?" says Ethel, shuffling through the classroom to reach Destiny's desk.

"Well, you knowI run a tutoring center, right?" Ethel nods. "I had applied for a government contract to run tutoring a program in local schools andI just found out we were awarded the contract."

"Oh, Destiny, that's amazing!" shouts Ethel, giving Destiny a big hug and crushing Destiny's letter between them. "Oh, my, but you are gonna be a busy gal, though. Your tutoring center and this government contract, teaching, and your PhD. You are the walking definition of Texas Big, my dear."

Ethel leaves as quickly as she came and Destiny is left standing there thinking Ethel is right. She *is* Texas Big and she *is* going to be busy. She is also going to need to hire more people for the center. There is going to be a lot of work to be done. Yet, she is so excited that the thought of everything she has to do pales in comparison. She tucks the letter in her bag and gets ready to start the day.

As her students file into the classroom, Destiny looks at them. She has worked hard with them the past couple of months, but they are a tough bunch of nuts to crack.

"Good morning, class," she says in greeting. Some of them reply with a mumbled good morning. "Can you all pass your homework assignments up to the front of the class, please?"

When she collects the homework assignments, Destiny sees that only about two-thirds of the class has handed in their assignments. Of the ones she has received, only half are fully completed.

She sighs as she puts the assignments on her desk and gets ready to start the lesson. She has spoken with a few of her students and she knows their home life isn't good. They have a really tough time at home, which makes it difficult to get homework done.

There has to be a way to help these kids. As she looks around the room, she thinks about it. After all, it's what she is good at, helping kids so they can reach their full potential. That's why she runs her tutoring center. That's why she teaches. And she is going to figure this out. She is going to find a way to help these kids.

"Okay, class. Get out your textbooks." Yes, she will get through to them.

When Destiny gets home after work that day, she finds her phone ringing as she walks through the door. She answers, "Hello?"

"Hi, Destiny. It's Dr. Brock calling."

"Oh, hi." Destiny had gone to see Dr. Brock a few days ago because she has been feeling tired lately. She thought maybe she was low on iron or something, so he did some blood tests.

"How are you feeling?" asks Dr. Brock.

"Pretty good. Still a bit tired."

"Well, I know why that is," says Dr. Brock. "You are going to have a baby."

"I... What?" says Destiny.

"You're pregnant, Destiny. About 12 weeks. That's why you have been feeling tired."

"Oh. Oh my!"

"Congratulations! I'll have Sheila call you soon with a date for a prenatal appointment."

"Um, yes, okay. Thank you so much. Goodbye."

Destiny hangs up the phone and just stands there. She is like a statue, leaning against the wall for support because she might fall over without it. She realizes she is holding her breath and she lets it out in one long sigh.

She pushes herself away from the wall and walks into the kitchen. She takes the leftover soup out of the fridge, puts it on the stove, and slices some fresh bread to go with it. She does everything in a daze.

A half an hour later, Destiny hears the front door open. She has been sitting nursing a cup of tea, waiting for Calix to come home. He is home for dinner and then he has to go back to work while there is still daylight.

"Destiny?" calls Calix. "You home?"

"Here, in the kitchen."

Calix walks in and says, "What's up?"

Destiny doesn't answer right away.

"Hey," says Calix. "Is everything alright? Did something happen?"

Destiny nods her head.

"What happened? Is it the family?"

Destiny nods again.

"Yours or mine?"

"Both," says Destiny.

"What? That doesn't make sense. Destiny what's wrong?"

Destiny looks up from her tea and smiles. "Calix, we're going to have a baby."

"A baby?"

Destiny nods a third time. Then Calix walks over, lifts Destiny out of her chair and gives her a huge hug, lifting her off her feet and swinging her around. "A baby!" he shouts.

Destiny hugs Calix back and they just stand hugging for a while, enjoying the thought of having a baby. Then Destiny lets go and they dish out soup and sit together to eat.

"Oh," says Destiny. "I have other good news. Get Your Mind Right Tutoring got the government contract."

"Congratulations!" says Calix. "But how are you going to be able to manage everything and a new baby?"

"I'll definitely have to hire more staff at the center. As long asI hire enough people, that will be fine. Everything else, well, I'll do the bestI can. It'll work out."

"Wait, when is the baby due?"

"I don't know," Destiny thinks for a moment. "I guess May or June."

"Well, then at least your first few weeks with the baby will be after the school year is out. That's good. Then we just have to figure out Florida in the summer."

"It'll work out.I know it will."

Calix takes his dishes to the sink. Then he comes over and kisses the top of Destiny's head. "I'm sure you're right," he says. "I have to get going back to work. You gonna be okay?"

"Well, of course," says Destiny. "I'm pregnant, not sick."

"And you are the most capable womanI know.I love you."

"I love you, too."

Calix leaves and Destiny cleans up the dinner dishes. Then she calls Momma. "Hello, Momma?"

"Destiny, what's wrong?"

"Nothing's wrong, Momma." She always thinks something is wrong when Destiny calls out of the blue. "I just have some news. Are you sitting down?"

"Yes, I am. Why?"

"Momma, I'm going to have a baby."

"Oh my! Oh my baby, my baby! Pop! Pop, you gotta come and hear this. Our little Destiny is gonna have a baby!"

"Hallelujah!" Destiny can hear Pop shouting in the background.

"Now, sugar," says Momma. "You gotta take care of yourself now, you hear? Eat well, get lots of sleep. And for Heaven's sake slow down. You do too much."

"I know, Momma. I will." Destiny thinks it is best not to tell Momma about the government contract. At least not yet.

They say goodbye and then Destiny goes upstairs to unpack a few boxes. While there, she looks in one of the spare rooms. This is the one she wants to be the nursery. She can picture it now, a bright yellow, pretty curtains, rocking chair by the window.

Destiny smiles. Then she goes downstairs, makes a cup of tea, and spends the rest of the evening reading research papers for her PhD. Well, trying to read. It's difficult to concentrate. By the time Calix gets home, she hasn't gotten much read because her mind has been wandering all evening. As she gets ready for bed, she thinks, *It'll all be just fine.*

Chapter 9

Student Success

One of Destiny's students, Marcus, makes his way down the court. The game is almost over and the score is tied. Marcus passes to another of her students, Devon, who goes in for the basket. He scores and the crowd erupts as the team converges on each other to celebrate in a group hug.

Destiny has made it out to most of the basketball games since Easter, despite her busy schedule and growing belly. She knows that showing her support for them in ways other than class work really impacts her relationship with them. When they feel closer to her and they know she truly cares, they feel more obligated to perform in class and do their very best.

This means that more and more homework assignments have been turned in, which has helped her students progress in their work. She is seeing good results in their homework and in their test results. Just thinking about it makes her smile.

And these boys, the ones on the basketball team, have really risen to the occasion. They have improved not only their class-work, but their performance and level of responsibility on the team. It is truly remarkable what a little genuine attention and interest can accomplish in youth.

The team is still gathered near the side of the court as Destiny stands up. She is sitting in the front row because she has no desire to climb the bleachers these days. She half walks, half waddles toward the team. She wants to congratulate them on their win. Marcus comes running up to her and gives her a high five and the other boys in her class follow suit.

"That was a great game, you guys," says Destiny.

"Thanks, Ms. Sycamores," says Devon. "We really rocked it."

"Yes, you did. AndI expect you to rock the homework that is due tomorrow, too."

"Yes, ma'am," the boys say in unison. Destiny smiles and leaves the gym. Time to gather her things and head home. She has a lot to do this evening. With the baby due in just a few short weeks, she wants to have everything organized so that she has as little as possible to do after the baby arrives.

The next morning, while she is checking her mail in the school office, Principal Brandfather pops her head out of her office. "Destiny, canI see you for a moment?"

"Sure thing," says Destiny.

Destiny goes in and Principal Brandfather says, "Sit, please."

Destiny wonders what this is all about. Principal Brandfather hasn't interacted with her much since she told her she was pregnant. Destiny gets the feeling that Principal Brandfather wasn't very happy about the news, despite the fact that her colleagues all congratulated her and even threw her a baby shower.

"The results of the state testing are in," says Principal Brandfather, her crisp white blouse and perfect pant suit a mirror of her demeanor. "AndI wanted to talk to you about the results from you students."

Little butterflies start fluttering in Destiny's stomach. Surely to goodness her students did a decent job on the test. She knows their marks have improved significantly in class. Yet, Destiny is worried Principal Brandfather is about to reprimand her for her class' poor performance.

"Did we do well?" asks Destiny, crossing her fingers, but dreading the answer.

Principal Brandfather looks at Destiny for a moment. "I know these students have been a challenge. Some of them had just dismal marks when you started working with them at the beginning of the year. Many of them didn't even care."

Oh boy, thinks Destiny, *this isn't going to be good.*

"But what you have managed to do with them is remarkable."

"What?" asks Destiny. "They did okay?"

"They did better than okay, Destiny. Out of all of your students 97% of them passed the state test."

"Really? Oh, that's wonderful!" Destiny is extremely relieved.

"Yes, it is. You have done such a good job with those students.I don't know how you did it, but the results are truly impressive. A number of your students got above 80%."

"I am so happy to hear that. They have worked very hard this year."

"Anyway," says Principal Brandfather, "I wanted you to know the results. You can share them with your class. They'll be happy to hear it."

Destiny gets the distinct feeling she is being dismissed. Even though Principal Brandfather is congratulating her, Destiny doesn't feel there is genuine warmth behind her words.

Destiny stands up. "Well, thank you.I appreciate it."

She heads up to her classroom, concerned by Principal Brandfather's detached behavior. But despite this, she is elated. Her class did well and she can't wait to tell them.

Twenty minutes later, Destiny watches as her students filter into the classroom. They take their seats and get organized, passing their homework to the front of the class as usual. They have gotten used to the routine Destiny has established, yet another reason they have improved so much over the year.

Once Destiny has collected all the homework assignments and has deposited them on her desk, she faces the class. The chatter dies down as they realize she is waiting for them. She tries very hard to look serious.

When they are quiet, Destiny says, "I was speaking with Principal Brandfather this morning. The results of the state tests are in."

Destiny can hear a couple of groans and a slight murmur ripple through the class as they shift uncomfortably in their seats.

Destiny continues. "Principal Brandfather wanted to share your results with me because of how remarkable they are."

"Remarkable?" asks Janelle. "Does that mean we did good?"

"Yes, it means you did well," says Destiny. The students clearly look relieved. "In fact, out of all the studentsI teach, 97% of you passed the test."

A cheer goes up from the students as they digest this news, although a couple of students still look worried. "But even more importantly," says Destiny, "I know that every one of you is doing well in class. Every one of you has improved. You have all been absolutely amazing."

Now everyone is smiling. "It's thanks to you, Ms. Sycamores," says Marcus.

"Well, thank you, Marcus. But to be honest, it is really because of you. You guys stepped up and did the work and you believed in yourself. That's what truly made the difference. I just pointed you in the right direction."

The class cheers again. "We should celebrate," says Janelle. "We should have a party."

"You know, that's a really good idea," says Destiny. The class begins to chatter again. Some people throw out ideas. They could dress up, have a theme, have pizza.

Destiny speaks above the rising tide of voices. "I think a pizza party would be a great idea. I need three students to help organize it. Who is willing to help?"

About a dozen hands go up and Destiny chooses three students, Janelle, Marcus, and Sharia. "You three can meet with me at lunch so we can discuss the party. And now, on with our class."

Groans erupt, but the students are all smiling and Destiny knows they are perfectly happy to get to work.

Chapter 10
Epilogue

Destiny sighs as she walks down the hall toward the staff room. It's the end of the day and she wants to touch base with Ethel before she leaves, but she can't track her down. Destiny is looking forward to sitting down and resting this evening. She might even watch some television. The baby is due in two weeks and she should already be off work, but this is the last week of school and she just doesn't want to miss it.

Destiny reaches out her hand to open the staff room door when she hears laughter inside. Then a woman's voice, it sounds like Rashema, says, "I heard Destiny's students did really well on the state test."

The other voice sounds like Richard. He says, "Well, it doesn't really matter what her results were."

"Why not?" asks Rashema.

"Because Brandfather doesn't like her. I don't know why, but Destiny is definitely not on her good side."

"That's ridiculous! Destiny is great. She's a fabulous teacher and she is such a nice person."

"Listen,I like her, too, but Brandfather doesn't.I wouldn't be surprised if she found a reason to get rid of Destiny, althoughI can't imagine what excuse she'd use."

"There is no way she could find one. Destiny is too good at what she does and her results are phenomenal."

"Well, at the very least, she wants Destiny out of a leadership position. At least that's whatI heard."

"From who?"

Destiny can't listen anymore. She turns and walks away, fuming. She doesn't even bother looking for Ethel anymore. She cannot believe what she just heard.

Destiny walks straight out of the school. She can't stand being in it for a moment longer. After everything she has accomplished, how can Principal Brandfather treat her this way? How on earth could Principal Brandfather have any issue with her? Anger, frustration, and hurt feelings rise up within Destiny and it is all she can do to keep from crying as she walks across the parking lot and gets into her truck.

When she does climb into her truck, Destiny just sits there. She is too paralyzed to do anything else. The emotions that were simmering beneath the surface boil over and she can feel the tears welling up. They spill out and run down her cheeks, leaving warm, wet trails.

All of a sudden, Destiny's vision fogs and she can see a large sign. It's a business sign hanging over a store front. It says iGlobal Educational Services. Then she is inside the door and she can see an expansive, two-floor office space. It is set up with a reception desk and various learning areas, each with a different focus. Students are working with instructors at the tables that are spread throughout the room.

Destiny knows that this is her business. This is what her tutoring business grows into—a large successful educational company that expands to help even more kids than she could ever have dreamed was possible.

It is her destiny to help others and it is obvious that she won't always do that through teaching at a school. It is also her destiny to not give others false hope, something she has been given time and time again in the education system.

No, her students and her tutoring clients will not get false hope from her. Every student who learns from her has the right to move into the rest of their life with a sense of self-worth, pride, and accomplishment, as well as a belief in themselves and what they are capable of.

Suddenly, Destiny is staring out the windshield of her truck again. She can see some other teachers approaching the parking lot so she starts her truck's engine, wipes the tears from her cheeks, and puts on her seatbelt.

As she drives out of the parking lot, she feels much better. If Principal Brandfather thinks she is going to get rid of or demote Destiny, she has another thing coming. Destiny has no plans to go anywhere, at least not for the time being. She knows she will leave the school system one day. And besides, she loves her students. They make working for a selfish principal bearable.

Plus, Destiny is about to have her first baby and then spend a wonderful summer in Fort Lauderdale, Florida, working on her PhD and spending time with her family. What could be better than that? Destiny turns on the radio and begins to tap her fingers on the steering wheel in time with the music listening to Yolanda Adam's "The Battle is Not Yours". Today is a great day.

www.ingramcontent.com/pod-product-compliance
Lightning Source LLC
Chambersburg PA
CBHW071204130626
46555CB00004B/1572